This edition published by Parragon Books Ltd in 2014 and distributed by

Parragon Inc.
440 Park Avenue South, 13th Floor
New York, NY 10016
www.parragon.com

ISBN 978-1-4723-3272-1

Printed in China

THE
LION KING

Bath • New York • Cologne • Melbourne • Delhi
Hong Kong • Shenzhen • Singapore • Amsterdam

As the morning sun rose high over the
African plain, animals and birds gathered
at the foot of Pride Rock.

"There he is!" one of them cried suddenly.
"There's the new prince!" Everyone cheered
and stamped their feet. "Welcome,
Prince Simba!" they shouted.

They watched in silence as Rafiki,
a wise old baboon, raised the lion cub high
in the air. The clouds parted and the sun's
rays shone down on the future king.
Slowly Rafiki lowered his arms and
took Simba back to his proud parents,
King Mufasa and Queen Sarabi.
It was a very special day.

Time passed quickly for little Simba. There was so much to learn. One morning, the king showed his son around the kingdom.

"Remember," Mufasa warned, "a good king must respect all creatures, for we exist together in the great Circle of Life."

Later that day, Simba met his uncle, Scar. The cub proudly told him that he had seen the whole of his future kingdom.

"Even beyond the northern border?" Scar asked slyly.

"Well, no," said Simba sadly. "My father has forbidden me to go there."

"Quite right," said Scar. "Only the bravest lions go there. An elephant graveyard is no place for a young prince."

Simba hurried away to find his best friend, a young lioness called Nala. Even though he knew it was wrong, Simba had decided to visit the elephant graveyard with Nala that very day.

He had no idea that Scar had ordered three hyenas to go to the elephant graveyard, too. Scar wanted them to kill Simba as the first step in his plan to take over Mufasa's kingdom.

Simba raced across the plains, leading Nala to
the forbidden place. Eventually they reached a pile
of bones and Simba knew they had arrived.

"It's creepy here," said Nala. "Where are we?"

"This is the elephant graveyard!" Simba cried. He was looking at a skull when he saw Zazu, his father's adviser.

"You must leave here immediately!" Zazu commanded. "You are in great danger."

But it was already too late! They were trapped. Three hyenas had surrounded them, laughing menacingly.

Simba took a deep breath and tried to roar—but only a squeaky rumble came out. The hyenas laughed hysterically.

Simba took another deep breath . . . **ROAARR!**

The three hyenas turned around to look into the eyes of—King Mufasa.

The hyenas fled, howling into the mist.

Mufasa sent Nala and Zazu ahead and walked slowly home with his son. "Simba, I'm disappointed in you. You disobeyed me and put yourself and others in great danger."

Simba felt terrible. "I was only trying to be brave like you," he tried to explain.

"Being brave doesn't mean you go looking for trouble," said the king gently.

The moon shone brightly above them and the stars twinkled in the dark sky.

Mufasa stopped. "Look at the stars! From there the great kings of the past look down on us. Just remember that they'll always be there to guide you, and so will I."

Simba nodded. "I'll remember."

By the next day, Scar had devised another plan to get
rid of Mufasa and Simba. He led Simba to the bottom
of a gorge and told him to wait for his father. Then the
hyenas started a stampede among a herd of wildebeest.

At that moment, Mufasa was walking along a ridge
with Zazu. "Simba!" he cried. "I'm coming!"

The king raced down the gorge and rescued his son,
but he could not save himself.

He fell onto an overhanging rock as the wildebeest swept by him. Looking up, he saw his brother.

"Scar, help me!" he cried. But Scar just leaned over and whispered, "Long live the king!" Then he pushed Mufasa into the path of the trampling wildebeest.

When the stampede was over Simba ran to his father's side.

"Father," he whimpered, nuzzling Mufasa's mane. But the king did not reply and Simba started sobbing.

"Simba," said Scar coldly, "what have you done? This is all your fault. The king is dead and you must never show your face in the pride again. Run away and never return."

As Scar returned to take the royal throne at Pride Rock for himself, Simba stumbled, tired and frightened, through the grasslands toward the jungle. He took a few more shaky steps and collapsed. Hungry vultures circled above him.

Eventually Simba opened his eyes. A warthog, called Pumbaa, and Timon, a meerkat, were gazing at him. They poured water into his dry mouth.

"You nearly died," said Pumbaa. "We saved you."

"Thanks for your help," said Simba, "but it doesn't matter. I've got nowhere to go."

"Why not stay with us?" said Timon kindly. "Put your past behind you. Remember! Hakuna matata—no worries! That's the way we live."

Simba decided to stay in the jungle with his new friends.

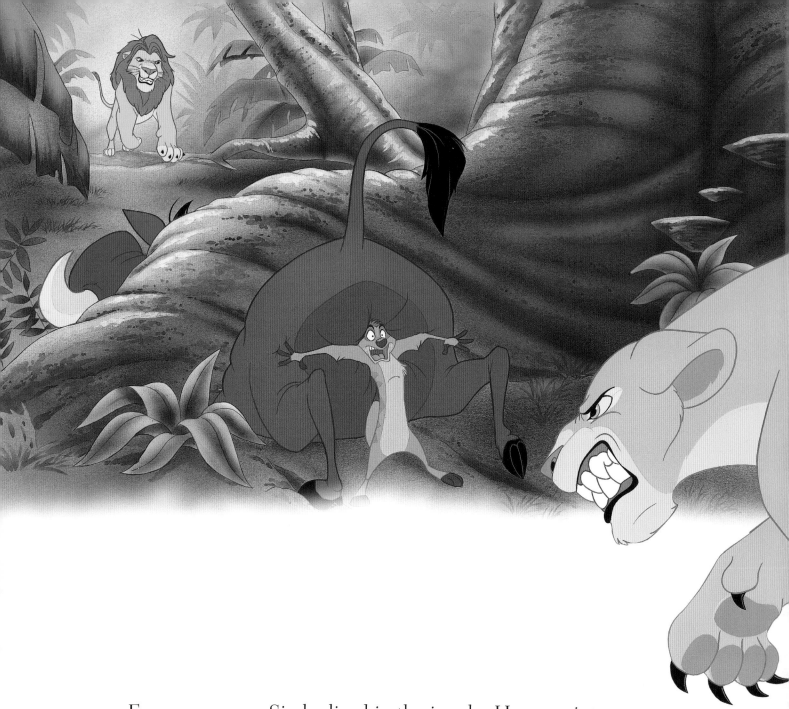

For many years, Simba lived in the jungle. He grew into a
strong lion. One day, he rescued Pumbaa from a hungry lioness—
it was Nala!

The two old friends were delighted to see each other again.
Nala told Simba about Scar's reign of terror at Pride Rock
and begged him to return. "With you alive, Scar has no right
to the throne," she said.

"I can't go back. I'm not fit to be a king," Simba said sadly.

"You could be," Nala told him.

Simba showed Nala his favorite places
in the jungle. "It's beautiful," she said.
"I can see why you like it—but it's not
your home. You're hiding from the future."
She turned and left her friend alone.

That night, Simba lay by a stream, thinking.
He heard a noise and looked up.

"Come with me," said Rafiki, "I will take you
to your father."

Simba followed him in wonder to the edge
of the stream. As Simba looked into the water,
his reflection gradually changed shape and
became his father's!

The reflection rose into the sky
and Simba heard Mufasa's voice:
"Simba. You must take your place
in the Circle of Life. You are my son
and the one true king." Then the
reflection, and Rafiki, disappeared.

Back at Pride Rock, the rains had been late in coming
and the land was dry. The hyenas paced impatiently around
King Scar.

"We're starving," they howled. "The herds have gone.
There's nothing left to eat."

Storm clouds gathered in the sky and a lightning
bolt scorched the earth. As the dry grass caught fire,
flames swept toward Pride Rock. A lion appeared
through the smoke. It was Simba!

Scar lunged at Simba, determined to keep his place as king. In the fierce battle that followed, Scar finally admitted that it had been him who had killed Mufasa. Simba heaved Scar over the cliff face. Simba was victorious!

Nala went to Simba's side.
"Welcome home!" she whispered.
As they smiled at each other, it started
to rain. The heavy drops soaked the
dry ground. The plains came back
to life, and soon, the herds returned.

One dawn, the animals and birds
made their way to the foot of Pride Rock.
Rafiki picked up a tiny cub. He showed
the son of King Simba and Queen Nala
to the cheering crowd below—they had
a new prince!

That night, Simba watched the stars rise
in the sky. "Everything's all right, father,"
he said softly. "You see, I remembered."
And the stars seemed to twinkle in reply.